Funny Bunnies

Robert Quackenbush

CLARION BOOKS

TICKNOR & FIELDS: A HOUGHTON MIFFLIN COMPANY

NEW YORK

For Piet

Clarion Books
Ticknor & Fields, a Houghton Mifflin Company
Copyright © 1984 by Robert Quackenbush

Printed in the U.S.A.

Library of Congress Cataloging in Publication Data

Quackenbush, Robert M.
Funny bunnies.

Summary: While little Lucy is out for a swim, various
bunnies from the staff crowd into her family's hotel
room.
[1. Hotels, motels, etc.—Fiction.   2. Rabbits—
Fiction]   I. Title.
PZ7.Q16Fu   1984   [E]   84-4314
ISBN 0-89919-267-X
P   10   9   8   7   6   5   4   3   2   1

Away on vacation,
the Bunny family
stopped at a hotel.
The only room left
was so tiny that
the door opened
into the hall.
But they took it
anyway.

While Mama and Papa Bunny
were busy unpacking,
little Lucy Bunny
went for a dip
in the hotel pool.

Came a knock
at the door.
Papa Bunny went
to see who
was there.

Two maids wanted in
to dust and sweep
the room.

Came another knock
at the door.
Papa Bunny
went to see
who was there.

A plumber wanted in
to fix the sink.

Came another knock
at the door.
Papa Bunny went
to see who
was there.

The plumber's helper
wanted in
with some pipe.

Came another knock
at the door.
Papa Bunny went
to see who
was there.

A janitor wanted in
to fix the lights.

Came another knock
at the door.
Papa Bunny went
to see who
was there.

A waiter,
thinking there was
a party going on,
wanted in
to take orders
for food and drinks.

Came another knock
at the door.
Papa Bunny went
to see who
was there.

A window washer
wanted in
to clean the window.

Came another knock
at the door.
Papa Bunny went
to see who
was there.

The waiter wanted in
to deliver the
food and drinks.

Just then,
little Lucy came back
from her swim
and opened the door.

Out tumbled
all the bunnies!

Little Lucy laughed
and laughed
and laughed
and said.....

...."What a bunch
of funny bunnies!"